car sickness ahead

oh, no! school nearby!

most boring road in the world!

especially ones in striped suits

C'mon, Mom, put the pedal to the metal

FEDERAL PRISON DO NOT STOP FOR HITCH-HIKERS

Amelia Hits the Road

by Marissa Moss
(and —YEEHAW— Amelia!)

I see the signs but I never see any deer on the road

watch out for cars on springs— BOING!

no reading backwards— ixnay!

Yippee— come and skip along it

State Hyway 74 Carefree Highway

absolutely no, don't even think about doing it!

Tricycle Press
Berkeley, California

ONE WAY

page turn ahead

This notebook is dedicated to
Brion,
who always listened to my stories, and
still does.

Mom's swim cap

I can't believe people still wear this kind of cap!

Cleo's bikini: she thinks she looks so hot in it.

Thank you, Jim Heimann of Los Angeles,
California, for letting me use your cool vintage travel map, circa 1937

good work, Tricycle!

→ TRICYCLE PRESS
P.O. BOX 7123
Berkeley, California 94707

Book Design by Amelia

thongs

shampoo

extra sock

and so much more!

cute travel sewing kit

Library of Congress Cataloging-in-Publication Data
Moss, Marissa.
Amelia Hits the Road / by Marissa Moss.
p.   cm.
Summary: Ten-year-old Amelia keeps a journal of the summer car
trip she takes with her mother and sister to Grand Canyon, Death Valley,
and their California hometown to visit Amelia's best friend.

ISBN 1-883672-83-X

[1. Diaries-Fiction 2. Automobile travel – Fiction.
3. Sisters–Fiction. 4. West (U.S.) – Fiction.]
I. Title
PZ7. M8535 Ah 1997
[Fic] – dc21   97-446
                                 CIP
An AMELIA Book   AC

First Tricycle Press Printing, 1997
Manufactured in Singapore

calamine lotion

this is how many bottles of beer on the wall

sun block

toothbrush

toothpaste

comb

brush

2   3   4   5   6   —   01   00   99   98

this is how many miles we went

chapstick

floss your teeth (on vacation?)

← bug off stuff

first aid kit – mostly aspirin

ok to pass
this direction

no passing this direction

This is my new  TRAVEL notebook. Mom bought it for me so I wouldn't be bored on the long driving part of this trip. She said if I'm busy writing, I won't be busy fighting with Cleo. I don't fight with Cleo. She fights with me.

Mom also packed:

lots of small boxes of cereal for breakfast

good for snacks, too

a stack of shiny new comic books - no schoolbooks, no homework, nothing educational

gum to keep Cleo from getting carsick - I'm the only kid whose sister is world famous for throwing up in the car

bags in case the gum doesn't work - yuk!

Then of course we have the regular trip stuff: calamine lotion, sunblock, bathing suits, clothes (with extra socks - Mom believes you always need extra socks, even in summer), shampoo, toothbrushes, toothpaste, dental floss, and books, books, and more books.

mom's box of paperbacks - she's panicked at the thought of being stuck anywhere without a book

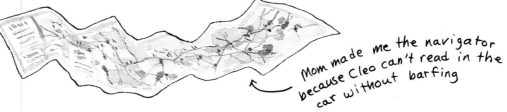

Mom made me the navigator because Cleo can't read in the car without barfing

Cleo can't fold maps, either

I'm an expert folder of course

This is going to be a LOOOOOOONG trip. We're going to the Grand Canyon, Death Valley, and Yosemite. Then comes the best part — I get to see Nadia again! I mean, even though we moved, she's <u>still</u> my best friend. We've been friends since kindergarten, and that's a long time. Now it's been almost a year since I saw her. (Writing letters and talking on the phone is <u>not</u> the same as being with someone.) I hope she still likes me in person. I wonder if she looks the same or if she's changed.

Nadia — before

Nadia — now

cool, shiny braces smile

eyes are happy to see me

is her hair short or long?

maybe she wears glasses now

hair this long

same smile? is she happy to see me?

at least her ears must be the same

me →

have I changed? I don't think so. I haven't even grown an inch!

this was a tricky position to draw, especially since I need one hand to hold my nose because of the putrid, purple stink

Oh, Baby, oh, marshmallow pie-ie ie-ie-ie-ie-ie! Oh, Baby, oh, spit in my eye-eye-eye-eye-eye-eye!

putrid purple

Cleo crud

Cleo, painting her toenails and screeching out a song

Being stuck in a car with Cleo is NOT my idea of fun. She stinks up the car with the smell of nail polish. She -BURPS- so loudly Mom jumps a foot off her seat. She turns up the air conditioner so high my teeth start chattering. And she sings the stupidest songs ever— off key, of course.

Mom says we should enjoy this togetherness. It seems like TOO much togetherness, if you ask me. Especially when Cleo gets carsick. Then the last thing in the world I want is to be together with her!

this car is definitely not big enough, we should put Cleo in a trailer behind the car

fumes—PU!

Cleo puking

all our junk piled up in back

me trying to get some fresh air

windows wide open

barf bag

mystery celebrity inside?

we also count cars, but only Bugs and limos score ↗

Today is the <u>longest</u> day of my life! Every minute takes about a year. Mom says it will be worth it once we get to the Grand Canyon. (But it will only be worth it if she pays me a million dollars!)

↑ our old home state

We've been playing the license plate game for hours (or decades!). By the time we get to the Grand Canyon, I bet I'll see <u>all</u> the states.

Last night Mom let me sit up front with her while Cleo snored in the back. Then it was cool to drive. I saw about a zillion stars, and the moon followed us. Even the roadside signs looked magical in the dark. I wish it could always be like that. (Especially the sleeping Cleo part.)

our new home state ↗

matchbook for my collection

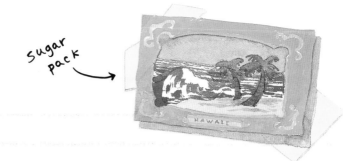
sugar pack

Driving was still booooring today, but at least we ate dinner at a great diner. The pumpkin pie was good, but the best part was the jukebox. It was a real old-fashioned one, all lit up, and you could see the records (not CDs!) drop. Cleo put a quarter in, and we danced together. It was fun! There were some great songs Mom remembered from when she was a kid. She thinks music today is terrible — but then, she's a mom.

cake in a cake stand, like it's a jewel or something

metal napkin holder — just try to get one napkin

me and Cleo dancing — Cleo even dipped me!

jukebox

caw-fee pot

floor like a chessboard

Jell-O cubes

grapefruit with a cherry so it looks fancy

thick mugs for hot chocolate with whipped cream on top

toilet gift wrap ↑

In the motel, I couldn't stop laughing. Cleo kept on cracking me up. When she saw the paper strip they put on the toilet seat, she acted like it was a present wrapped up for her.

We opened all the drawers, tried all the TV channels, and inspected the closet. It was too late to go swimming in the pool, but the Bible in the nightstand drawer gave me a great idea — Cleo and I wrote funny notes to leave in all the dresser drawers.

A surprise for me? You shouldn't have! It's tooo much! At last, a place to throw up. No more bags for me.

wrapper
flusher

I guess Cleo doesn't like puking any more than I like seeing (and smelling) her puke →

PU! Don't put stinky socks in this drawer!

Didn't your mother teach you to fold your clothes NEATLY!?

Did you flush the toilet? Did you wash your hands?

Beware of chewing gum left in drawers — yuuuch!

No eating chips in bed!

"A peanut sat on a railroad track..."

Peanuts in History 22¢

Famous Felines 6¢

Frank Jr.

Pinky

Presidential Dogs 12¢

I wrote postcards to Nadia and Leah before I went to bed. Nadia says she's glad I met Leah and have a new friend, but I wonder, does that mean she has a new friend, too?

Approved MOTEL
TOURIST HOME

Here's what I wrote

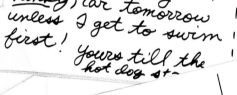

FEENY'S MOTEL
Drive in and dive in!

Dear Leah,
   This is the motel we're staying at tonight. I didn't get to swim in the pool because we got here too late, but no way I'm sitting in that hot, sticky (and stinky) car tomorrow unless I get to swim first!
       Yours till the hot dog st—

Headgear through the ages

TOP HAT

Leah Feinberg
2282 Lomo
Oopa, Oregon
97881

ABURGER

Motel

Hungry Hamburger
— clean your plate!

Dear Nadia,
   It feels great to be out of the car! So far the most interest-ing thing I've seen on this trip is the pool here. At least Cleo only threw up once today. (She's the Barf Queen!)

CARD COMPANY

LITERARY WHALES

Nadia Kurz
61 South St.
Barton, CA
91010

Yours till UDK,
Amelia
(P.S. I can't wait to see you!)

The Place to — When You
STOP   GO

Drive in
and dive in.

mouse trap

drain trap →

trap door
floor
tourist trap

corny roadside reptile zoo — 2 lizards and 1 snake

I like staying in motels, I like eating in restaurants, but all this driving, driving, driving is driving me crazy! We sang every song we could think of — "Found a Peanut", "On Top of Old Smoky", "Down by the Banks of the Hanky Panky", "The Bear Went over the Mountain", "Goofy Grimy Gopher Guts" — until Mom screamed at us to

STOP!

Then Cleo started reading every sign we passed until I hit her to shut her up and she hit me back so I hit her again and Mom yelled at us some more.

I asked Mom if she was enjoying all this togetherness. She just glared at me.

Eat at Joe's
Passing Lane
Ahead G... F...

So when we saw the billboard that said:

> MYSTERIOUS PLACE
> 30 MILES AHEAD
> Stop and Experience the Mystery!

I begged Mom to stop. She said forget it, it's just a junky tourist trap. The next sign said:

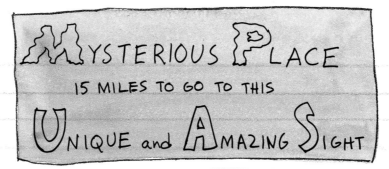

me in high begging gear

Please please please please please please please please please please please pretty please with sugar and whipped cream and sprinkles and chocolate chips and a cherry on top — pleeeeeeeeeeease!

I really begged. I needed to get out of that car! I guess Mom did too, because when we came to the next sign:

she said, "Well, maybe we could use a break to stretch our legs." And when we came to the last sign:

she pulled in and stopped.

decal you're supposed to put on your car window (Mom says it's to advertise you were enough of a jerk to stop) →

I'VE EXPERIENCED THE MYSTERIOUS PLACE
?

What we saw next was so astounding I'm not sure I can write about it. The Mysterious Place was — indescribable. At least, I can't describe it, but Mom's word for it was "cheesy" — and she didn't mean cheddar.

ball rolls UP hill — defying forces of gravity!

↑ wooden slide built into hill

For this we paid $8 plus $1 for parking — what's mysterious is why anyone would give money to see this!

Some wonder! Really the slides are downhill. They just look uphill because of the slope of the ground and the path we were on. Duh!

↑ Cleo, completely amazed — she has to take a picture of this wonder

↑ Mom, completely disgusted

pom poms with feet and jiggly eyes glued to a magnet — ooh, how cute!

They went to the MYSTERIOUS PLACE and all I got was this shirt

↑ joke T-shirts

The truly mysterious place was the gift shop, where there was an astonishing display of junk. I couldn't believe anyone would buy that stuff. All I wanted was a soda, but Mom said she wasn't paying those high prices, and I didn't want to waste my own money.

Genuine BUFFALO CHIPS

joke snacks

↑ mystery caps

At least we got out of the car for a while,

Cleo wasted her money in the gift shop on some tarot cards — how mysterious!

When Cleo told my fortune with her new cards she said I would visit new places and meet new people. DUH! I knew that without a tarot deck. I wanted to tell her fortune, but she wouldn't let me touch her stupid cards. Anyway, I know what her fortune is: you will get a big pimple right on your nose, and everyone will stare at it.

magic eight ball — answers all questions

Cleo said I drooled when I fell asleep in the car. I DID NOT! But I did have a terrible dream. I was at Nadia's house, but when I opened the door, some other kid lived there. What a nightmare!

tea leaves — reveal the past, show the future

When I woke up, we weren't at Nadia's house, but we were at the Grand Canyon. Finally! Seeing it for real, not on TV or in pictures, was like a dream, a good one. I mean, it was familiar, but completely different, too.
　　　　First of all, it's . . . .

palm reading — you hold your life in your hands

Ouija board — the spirit speaks!

Cleo believes in all this stuff — I'm not sure if I do or not

It's so ENORMOUS it's like going to an entirely different planet. As far as you can see, there it is. And besides being HUGE, it is so old. I felt like I was looking back in time, to prehistoric earth. I mean, it took FOREVER for the river and wind to make such deep channels. Mom says the Grand Canyon is the Earth's old-age wrinkles, like the lines on her forehead. (Nice try, Mom.)

  Cleo said it was just a big hole in the ground, why bother to come, but I thought it was awesome!

It was too late to hike, but the night was beautiful anyway. I've never seen so many stars in my <u>life</u>. I just sat outside our cabin and stared at the stars. It made me dizzy! Cleo showed me some constellations. I knew the Big Dipper and Orion before, but now I know Taurus and Gemini, too.

I can find the stars that make Gemini, but I can't see twins in this

↑ constellations are like giant dot-to-dots, but once you connect the dots, you still have to imagine the picture

Orion →

← I can see this picture pretty easily—except for the legs

Taurus is really hard to see, but its eye is really bright, so that's what I looked for

I love to think that people saw and named those same stars thousands of years ago! But Cleo said that the stars we see might not even be there any more because they're <u>so</u> far away that it takes <u>years</u> for light to travel from that particular star to my eye. I mean, I could see a star now that's already novaed (is that a word? Should I say went nova? Blew up? Exploded? Imploded? Outploded?). I can't think about that — it's <u>too</u> ~~wierd~~ ~~weird~~ ~~wierd~~ ~~weird~~ ~~wierd~~ weird!

AGGH! I <u>HATE</u> this word! ↗

We got up early to see the Grand Canyon at sunrise (a major accomplishment for Cleo). It was spectacular — all orange and pink and yellow.

I can't imagine being the first person who saw all this. Especially because the land coming up to the edge is just ordinary, and then suddenly there's this amazing THING.

ordinary tree

← unsuspecting tourist

ordinary grass

← that first step is a doozy!

After breakfast, we hiked down the Kaibob Trail to Cedar Ridge. It was already hot, hot, HOT, and Cleo was whining, whining, WHINING, so I went ahead to get away from her. But I couldn't get away from the mule poop. Lazy people ride mules up and down the trail, and they poop everywhere (the mules, not the people), so I had to dodge stinky plops constantly.

why don't they just tie bags to the mule's tail to catch all the poop?

↑ mule

mule diaper

dust waiting to be kicked up ↑

mule plop obstacle course — ooops!

before hike ←
↑ sparkling white tennies

after hike ↓
dusty pink tennies ↗

The good part was being <u>inside</u> the canyon — definitely cool (even though it was hot). And I met a boy. His name is Mako. We hiked together the whole way. Mako is from Japan, and he's really nice. Cleo acted like a jerk, of course, saying how cute Mako is. Maybe he's a little cute, but mostly he's just fun to talk to, and I'd rather hike with him than Cleo <u>any</u> <u>day.</u>

Mako said there's nothing like the Grand Canyon in Japan. He took lots of pictures to show his friends. He even took a picture of me!

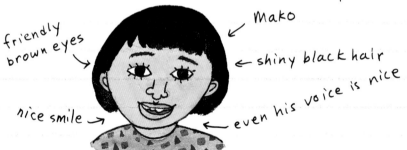
friendly brown eyes →
← Mako
← shiny black hair
even his voice is nice
nice smile →
← even his voice is nice

We traded addresses so we can be pen pals.

Mako showed me how to write his name in Japanese — it's hard to do — I hope I got it right →

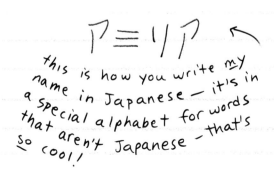
↖ this is how you write my name in Japanese — it's in a special alphabet for words that aren't Japanese — that's <u>so</u> cool!

↑ chain of gum wrappers Mako gave me — he's an expert at this — once he made a chain 4 feet long!

I wanted to get dreamcatcher earrings like this so I could catch good dreams and keep out the bad ones, but Mom said they were too expensive and I don't have pierced ears anyway (well, not yet) — so Cleo bought them for her friend Gigi (lucky Gigi!)

Maybe someday he'll even visit me like I'm going to visit Nadia.

I wanted to get Nadia something special from the gift shop, and I found the perfect thing. It's a pair of dolls. Nadia can pick which one she wants, and I'll keep the other one. My doll will remind me of Nadia, and her doll will remind her of me!

← the dolls look like this

the tag on them looks like this ↓

Leah's rocks look like these (but I'm keeping a few) ↓

Certificate of Authenticity
Handmade by
Native Americans
Artist: _____
Artist#: 113.697

↑ Thanks, Artist # 113.697!

For Leah I got some beautiful stones, shiny and all colors.

Mom said we only had time for one last look at the Grand Canyon. It was all purple and red with long shadows. Every time we look at it, it's different. I wonder what it will be like if I come back when I'm grown up. Less mule poop, I hope.

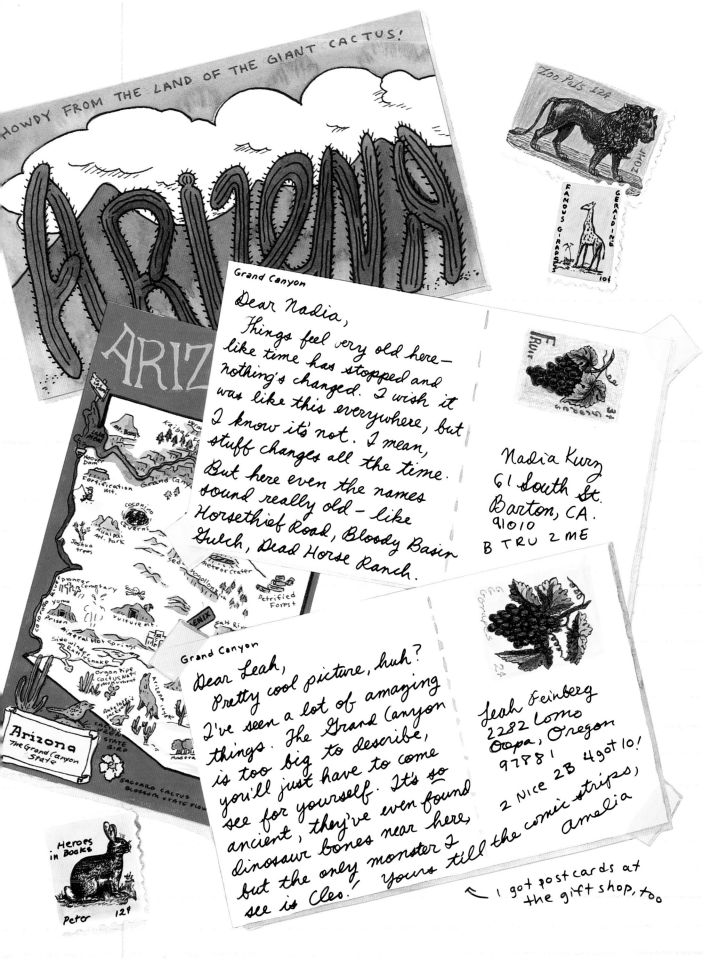

HOWDY FROM THE LAND OF THE GIANT CACTUS!

ARIZONA

Zoo Pals 12¢

FAMOUS GIRAFFE
GERALDINE 10¢

ARIZ

Mt. Baldy
Lake Mead
Kaibab Forest
Hoover Dam
Fortification Mt.
Grand Canyon
Coconino Caverns
Hualpai Mt. Park
Joshua trees
Pioneer Cemetery
Colorado Yuma Prison
Meteor Crater
Mogollon Rim
Petrified Forest
PHOENIX
Salt River
Mineral Hot Springs
Sidewinder Rattlesnake
Vulture mt.
Organ Pipe Cactus Nat'l Monument
Antelope
Arizona toad
Cactus Wren

Arizona
The Grand Canyon State

STATE BIRD

SAGUARO CACTUS
BLOSSOM STATE FLOWER

Grand Canyon

Dear Nadia,
Things feel very old here—
like time has stopped and
nothing's changed. I wish it
was like this everywhere, but
I know it's not. I mean,
stuff changes all the time.
But here even the names
sound really old – like
Horsethief Road, Bloody Basin
Gulch, Dead Horse Ranch.

F
Russ
MADEIRA 3¢

Nadia Kurz
61 South St.
Barton, CA.
91010
B TRU 2 ME

Grapes
2¢

Grand Canyon

Dear Leah,
Pretty cool picture, huh?
I've seen a lot of amazing
things. The Grand Canyon
is too big to describe,
you'll just have to come
see for yourself. It's so
ancient, they've even found
dinosaur bones near here,
but the only monster I
see is Cleo! Yours till the comic strips,
2 Nice 2B 4got 10!
Amelia

Leah Feinberg
2282 Lomo
Oopa, Oregon
97881

Heroes
in Books
Peter 12¢

← I got postcards at
the gift shop, too

← sarsparilla

← old-fashioned candy jars with old-fashioned candy with funny-sounding names

← horehound drops

← this pump has personality!

GAS

Every day on this trip it feels like we're going back in time. We stopped at a store that was also a gas station, and the pumps were old-fashioned and rounded. They reminded me of a cartoon where everyone wears gloves so they have sausage fingers. Hands look friendly and funny that way, and so did the gas pump, not like the blah gas pumps we have now.

Mom says sometimes when things change, they get worse, not better. But she's not always right. She only likes old music. And, besides, I've seen her high school pictures — talk about dorky clothes!

macrame purses

long hair parted in the middle for boys and girls

hip huggers, some with bell bottoms, some not

bell bottoms

platform shoes

a singer mom used to like wore shoes with a goldfish in each heel — how did he feed them? Your what if they died? feet would smell like rotting fish — PU!

clunky peace necklaces with leather ropes

boy (or is it girl?)

girl (or is it boy?)

tumble-weeds a-tumblin' ↘

We had a picnic at a ghost town. No one had lived there for a LOOOONG time. There used to be a silver mine, so people rushed there to get rich. When the silver ran out, they all left. The buildings looked like they were holding their breath, waiting for the people to come back. I thought I would find some treasure or old coins, but I didn't.

LUCY DILL
She was a dilly.
1848-1891

R.I.P.
Pa Guffy
He took to his bed, and there he stayed, till in this grave, he was laid.

Here lies Silver Pete With his saddle At his feet
~1886~

Crackshot Ed until he met Straight Shot Bill

↖ the cemetery behind the town had some interesting tombstones — some even told stories

Cleo found a bone. She said it was from a dead miner. Mom said it was a chicken bone from someone's picnic, but Cleo's keeping that bone like it's something special. She's going to write Gigi about it, and when we get home, they'll use the Ouija board to discover the bone's true identity.

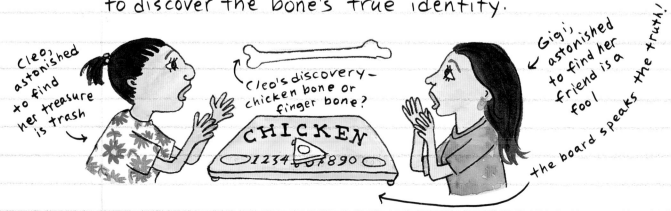

Cleo, astonished to find her treasure is trash →

Cleo's discovery — chicken bone or finger bone?

CHICKEN
1234567890

Gigi, astonished to find her friend is a fool ↙

the board speaks the truth!

cactus holding a hot dog

cactus with a bumpy nose

cactus wearing a skirt

cactus with a hairdo

We drove past miles and miles of cactus and tumbleweed, but no skeletons or bones (except Cleo's find). I thought we'd see something, but it was just a lot of nothing.

in movies you always see bones bleaching in the desert

Finally, after I'd asked "Are we THERE yet?" at least a zillion times, we came to this big castle. It was like a mirage, but it was real. Mom stopped the car (yeah!) and said, "Welcome to Death Valley." I thought for sure we'd see skeletons in Death Valley, but all we saw was a grave.

I couldn't draw all of the buildings— it was too big

we went on a tour of the castle, and there is a skeleton buried there, but we didn't get to see it

this is → someone else's grave and it wasn't near the castle

shorty

← Scotty's castle — some guy built it for a vacation home — it'd be a great place for a vacation, except it's hot, hotter, HOTTEST! no one smart goes to Death Valley in the summer, and I know why!

← squirrel prints

I didn't see this snake (phew!) — a sidewinder — but I saw its tracks all over the dunes

antelope squirrel — I saw one near Scotty's castle

this isn't a tiny kangaroo — it's a kangaroo rat — more tracks I saw in the sand dunes

tail print

snake footprints

It is really beautiful here. I just wish my clothes were air-conditioned. Near where we're staying there are miles and miles of sand dunes, but no beach. The waves of sand are like a dry frozen ocean. I would have built a sand castle, but I could only stand to be out of the car for 10 minutes before I felt like I was baking in a giant oven.

me surfing a sand wave

Then, in the middle of the desert, there's all this hard, dried-out salt, like there was once an ocean here. This place is so mixed up!

this raven really startled me — it had a sharp beak and glossy black feathers like a crow, but it was HUGE!

Cleo sprinkled some of that salt on her hard-boiled egg at our picnic lunch so she could say she'd eaten Death... Valley

rocks, sand, and more rocks and sand →

Badwater

↖ you aren't behaving, you bad water!

There are rocks and mountains, too. The best part is their names.

Death Valley devil ↘

Artist's Palette →

dip your brush in! ↓

BONK!

these rocks are made from volcanic ash and really are these colors →

Devil's Cornfield ↓

just dust and dirt - no corn

I'd break my beak on that corn.

Devil's Dishes ↘

Devil's Toilet ↗
(just kidding!)
really these are sulphur springs - PU! - smells like rotten eggs or Cleo after she's been out in the hot sun awhile

a cactus would be the Devil's chair ↗

Mom says the desert is peaceful because it's so big and open. And quiet. I've never heard such LOUD quiet as here.   Of course, Cleo says it's driving her crazy, but I like it. I wish Cleo would just stay in the hotel and paint her toenails if she's going to whine. All she does is drink soda and burp anyway. How can I hear the quiet with all her burping?

Outside of Death Valley, it still feels old and dusty and quiet. There are old mine shafts cut into the hills, and when we drive through towns, it's like no one lives in them. The yards are full of old rusting junk.

We hadn't gone very far when, even without me nagging, Mom stopped the car at one of those historical markers. It said we were in a place called Manzanar, where 10,000 Japanese-Americans lived during World War II. It was like a camp for war prisoners, only these people weren't enemy soldiers, just regular people — kids even! But since the U.S. was fighting Japan, our government thought even Japanese-Americans were bad. I can't believe a president could be so stupid. (I hope he got a lot of angry letters!)

i'm mad!

barbed wire — it used to be all around the camp — it reminds me of when all the caution tape was up at school after the fire

I can't believe it really happened, but you can still see some guard posts and a cemetery with Japanese writing on the gravestones. Miss Know-It-All Cleo says she studied about Manzanar in social studies, but no one ever told me. I wonder if Mako knows.

I thought Mom would give us one of her "See how lucky you are" lectures, but she didn't.

all the rusted-out junk we passed seemed even sadder after Manzanar

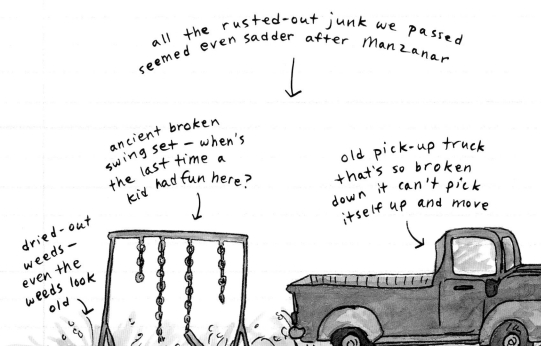

ancient broken swing set — when's the last time a kid had fun here?

old pick-up truck that's so broken down it can't pick itself up and move

dried-out weeds — even the weeds look old

Cleo bought a little fan in Death Valley and now she won't leave the car without it — I hope it clips off the tip of her jelly roll nose!

We've seen a lot of strange things on this trip (besides Cleo in a bikini — gross!). Today we stopped at Mono Lake.

now this was a real Mysterious Place!

sand ooze

mono Lake rock thing

bird poop

It has all these crumbly rock sculpture-like formations. They look just like sand when you ooze it through your hands at the beach, only bigger (and harder). I wonder how all these different kinds of places get made.

This has been a great trip, except for two things — all the driving and Cleo! I've watched her paint her nails, sing off-key, throw up, chew food with her mouth open, burp, crack her knuckles, and pick her nose.

I CAN'T STAND IT ANYMORE!

I couldn't help it. When Mom said it was time to get back in the car and head for Yosemite, Cleo started her usual whining chant.

I didn't yell. I didn't hit (though I wanted to do both). But I _did_ take my can of soda and I _did_ pour it over Cleo's head. Man, did that feel good!

Mom said no TV for me tonight at the motel, but it was _definitely_ worth it.

a new sugary-sweet hairdo ↓

same old sour personality

Cleo after her soda shower →

Cleo pouted all the way to Yosemite – too bad!

I wasn't sure our car would make it, because the road went up and up and up through the gray Sierra Mountains. If Cleo didn't eat all those hamburgers, the poor car wouldn't have to work so hard.

← lady using blow-dryer on her curlers while watching TV and blabbing

Then after all the grayness, we came out into Tuolumne Meadows, and we were in Yosemite! It was just like when Dorothy lands in Oz after being in black-and-white Kansas. It was amazing! Even Cleo couldn't stop smiling — the feeling of being someplace really special was so strong.

Cleo acting like she's in The Sound of Music

I almost ran into a deer — it looked right at me

we got out of the car to run through this meadow full of wild flowers — the grass was so high, you could almost play hide-and-seek in it

Then we drove down into Yosemite Valley, past all these great rocks (I mean GREAT) and waterfalls. It was beautiful, but it definitely wasn't peaceful. It was CROWDED — people yakking, radios blaring, even TV sets blasting away from all the RVs.

bear warning sign – keep all food out of reach of bears →

special trash cans to keep bears out →

canned food-yum!

↑ bear looking for a snack

But once we started hiking above the Valley, we got away from the roller-bladers, the bikes, and the crowds. We still had Cleo, though.

this is the view from Glacier Point →

postcard from the valley store ↗

We hiked up Lambert Dome, and we could see **ALL** around for miles. I felt like I was floating on a cloud over all these mountains.

That was tasty, just like a hamburger. BURP.

Cleo chanted "A million bottles of beer on the wall" on the hike back, but I just ran ahead so I wouldn't have to hear her. No way is she going to ruin Yosemite for me!
I hope a mountain lion eats her.

Bridalveil Fall — the water is so loud, it drowns out Cleo — great!

Half Dome — it looks like a scoop of ice cream (but it's not really pink) →

we saw some people climbing this smoooooth rock with ropes — it looked impossible, but they were doing it

Only a little more togetherness, and I'll be :FREE: of Cleo, at least for a little while. Tomorrow we go to Nadia's!

I'm excited, but I'm nervous, too. Will Nadia still like me? Or do I have a picture of her in my head that's not true anymore, like the stars I see but aren't really there? If I think about it too much, I'll get a stomachache.

BIG rock ←

tiny car →

El Capitan — I salute you!

boy's house

boy gets to fly all by himself ↓

grandparents' house →

The Visit

A boy visited his grandparents every year. They lived far away so he couldn't see them more than that. When they saw him, they always said, "Oh, you've grown so much! Look how you've changed!" But the boy felt exactly the same. Finally, one year, he noticed that they were the ones who were changing. His grandma had more white hair.

grandma's wrinkly prune face →

← wispy white hair

← boy

six hairs left →

grandpa's old leathery face ←

His grandpa had almost <u>no</u> hair. And they both had lots more wrinkles. That scared him because he knew they were getting <u>very</u> old and could die any minute. That visit was the first time the boy felt he had changed, too, just like they said. He did feel older, but not better, just sadder. He hugged his grandparents very tight.

<u>That</u>'s not a good story. That's a <u>terrible</u> story! Am I worried that Nadia has wrinkles and is going to die? That is SO ridiculous! She's only TEN years old!

 ## A Change for the Better

A girl got a puppy for her birthday. She named him Tuffy T. Bone (or Tuffy for short). He was very cute, but also very wild. He pooped and peed everywhere. He chewed up her new shoes (and the rug and the chair and the curtains and the doormat).

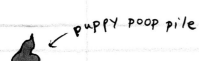
← puppy poop pile

puppy pee puddle →
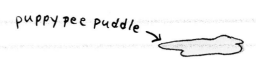

He ate up her homework (and of course the teacher didn't believe her, even though she was telling the truth).

But, after a while, he got bigger. He wasn't as cute, but he didn't pee on the girl's things anymore, and he was a very good friend. He would go on walks and catch frisbees and curl up next to the girl when she did her homework. Sometimes she missed having a puppy, but mostly she loved having a dog.

← same store on the corner

← same newspaper rack

← same potholes in the street

↑ same plastic flamingos in the yard of the purple house (still purple)

Now that we're back in our old city, everything looks so familiar. Our old neighborhood, even our old house, is exactly the same, only it's not home anymore. When we parked in Nadia's driveway, I was SO nervous my hands were all sweaty.

our ex-home
↓

the same as when we lived here, except there's a tricycle in the front yard — another kid must live here now

↑ same old glowing doorbell

I rang the doorbell and it seemed like forever but at last she opened the door — the same old Nadia with her same old smile, only NO BRACES!

She said, "Surprise! Now you see the real me." We looked at each other grin, grin, grinning, and then we hugged. It felt great!

same gingery shampoo smell

Nadia now
↓

no haircut

still no glasses

same happy-to-see-me smile, but no more zipper teeth

another change — she got her ears pierced, she even owns 4 pairs of earrings!

wearing the necklace I made for her

Nadia put the doll on her shelf with all her special stuff

giant seashell her grandma gave her

blown glass animal collection

jewelry box with little lock and key

miniature books collection

pretty rock

I let her pick which doll she wanted. She picked the girl, and she's going to name her Amelia =! I can tell she really likes it, but next time, I'm getting her earrings.

And she had a present for me — it was a notebook of all the stories she's written. I can't wait to read them

the first story is called "Best Friends"

Nadia's notebook (now it's my notebook — to read, not to write)

Nadia's room is just the way I remembered, except she has new drawings tacked to her bulletin board, the postcards I sent her — and a certificate with a ribbon for winning the Young Authors' Faire!

Nadia's bedroom

ceiling

stick-on stars that glow in the dark

bulletin board

special things shelf

desk piled with papers, books, pencils, pens, stickers, and stuff

lamp

door

wall socket

fuzzy warm bunny slippers

postcards from me

Young Authors' Faire
Nadia Kury
has been awarded
First Place
for excellence in writing

old school photo of me →

authors' faire certificate

blue ribbon

COUNT DOWN TO AMELIA
10 9 8
6 5 4 3
2 1 A

MAP OF A'S ROUTE

new drawings

Nadia's bulletin board

notes Nadia writes to herself to remind her of important things — like my visit!

I asked her why she hadn't told me that she won, and she turned all pink (I forgot how pink she gets when she blushes). She said she didn't want me to feel bad because I hadn't won. But I didn't feel at all bad. In fact, I felt great! Nadia is a true friend to think of my feelings first, and I'm not jealous — well, maybe a little, but only of her earrings, not of her winning the Young Authors' Faire.

Nadia's earrings — one set looks like cute little grapes

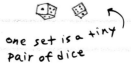

one set is a tiny pair of dice

I felt even better when she pulled out the Experiment Kit I sent her for her birthday. She saved it to do with me, just like she said she would!

But then she asked if I still wanted to do it with her. I said of course I do, why wouldn't I? And she said she thought I might have changed and maybe I wasn't interested in science anymore.

test tubes
test tube holder

poisonous chemical- watch out!
something oxide
chrom- ium dadada
Boric ladi- da
Sodium some- thing
← chemicals →

tongs to hold test tube with

funnel

measuring beaker

little metal spoon to measure chemicals with

instruction booklet so you can make your own Frankenstein monster

beaker

litmus paper

simple experiment #1: Take a paper cup. Cut a hole in the bottom. Turn upside down and seal opening (not hole) with foil. Put a big spoonful of baking soda in the foiled bottom of the cup. In a beaker, mix vinegar (maybe half a cup) with red food coloring. Pour the mixture into the foiled cup. Watch it froth over — it's a volcano!

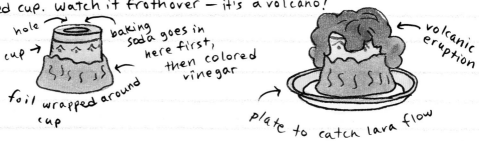

hole
cup →
baking soda goes in here first, then colored vinegar
foil wrapped around cup
volcanic eruption
plate to catch lava flow

So all this time I had been worrying about Nadia changing, and she was thinking the same thing about me. But I haven't changed at all—no pierced ears, no new smile, nothing. But I asked Nadia, anyway, if she thought I'd changed.

And she said YES!

I couldn't believe it. How? How? How? I had to know!

At first she wouldn't answer me. Then she said, "I don't know. It's just that first you moved away and met all these new people, and I stayed here. Then you went on this great trip and saw all kinds of cool stuff, and I haven't gone anywhere. You have to tell me everything!"

wide open spaces

wide open road

Death Valley

Mako

Grand Canyon

Mysterious Place

Manzanar

Mono Lake

Yosemite

me

Dancing with Cleo

She's right! I have changed.

     And I did have a lot to tell her. I said it was going to be like the last time I slept over, when we talked till 4 in the morning.
     "Yeah," said Nadia. "Some things never change."

     She was right again.